STORYTIME

TOM THUMB

Retold by
MAE BROADLEY

Illustrated by
ANNA DZIERZEK

TOM THUMB

Many, many years ago, England was ruled by a great king whose name was Arthur. He was a wise and a just king and all the country prospered under his rule.

To the court of King Arthur came the greatest musicians and the cleverest scholars, the bravest knights and the wisest counsellors. And, especially near and dear to the king, there was a magician of marvellous powers called Merlin.

But Merlin did not remain close to Arthur all the time. For this man of magic knew that the power of kings came not from their courtiers but from the common people who had never been inside the palace gates. If he would continue to be great, Arthur must know the hopes and the fears of all his subjects. And so that he might keep his king well informed, Merlin, disguised as a poor traveller, would wander round the countryside talking to the people and living in their homes.

So it was that one day he visited the home of a humble peasant and his wife. Taking him to be a poor beggar, they shared their humble meal with him willingly.

They were good people, thought Merlin, as he talked with them. He admired the well-scrubbed neatness of their home and the well-tended orderliness of their small farm. Yet, even while they smiled, he sensed their deep sadness. This was not good; all the subjects of King Arthur should be happy and content.

"You have a good life together," Merlin addressed the couple. "Your home is comfortable, you have enough to eat and few worries. Why, then, are you both so unhappy?"

"Oh, indeed, we have a lot to be thankful for, and a lot more than most people," said the farmer's wife. "But the years go by and still we have no children. If only we had a child no bigger than my thumb we would be the happiest couple in the land."

No bigger than my thumb . . . the idea amused the mighty Merlin. Could it be done, he wondered . . .

" I can see no reason why you shouldn't have your wish," he laughed, and he walked out of the house, leaving the poor couple staring in amazement after him.

Later, by the power of the great Merlin, the couple did have a child, a little boy who was perfect in every way and as bright and intelligent as any parents could wish . . . but he was no more than two inches high. So they christened him Tom Thumb.

The tiny fellow was a great joy to his parents, whose only problem now was how to clothe him, for human hands could not sew such tiny clothes as he would need.

Their problem came to the ears of the queen of the fairies. Curious to see the little boy, she visited the farm the next day.

"You should be very happy to have such a beautiful little boy," she told Tom's parents. "And I shall be delighted to have my own tailors make him the finest clothes."

An oak leaf had he for his crown;
His shirt of web by spiders spun;
With jackets wove of thistledown,
His trousers were of feathers done.
His stockings of apple rind they tie
With eyelash from his mother's eye;
His shoes were made of mouse's skin,
Tanned with the downy hair within.

Tom Thumb was very proud of his splendid costume, nor did his lack of size daunt him; he strutted round the countryside like a giant.

He was a lively boy, always merry and full of pranks. And, despite his small size, he was often useful to his father on the farm.

There was a day when his father decided to clear some woodland.

"I wish there was someone who could bring the cart through the woods for me," he remarked to his wife.

"Let me do it," piped up Tom Thumb.

"Why, a little fellow like you couldn't drive the cat, let alone the big farm horse," laughed his mother.

"Just put me into the horse's ear and I promise I'll take him straight to my father," said Tom, when the time had come for his father to want the cart.

His mother did as he asked, more to amuse the boy than because she believed he could do as he said.

But clever Tom whispered into the old horse's ear, guiding him safely through the woods.

Tom's spirit of adventure often got him into trouble. There was the time when he dived into the goldfish bowl for a swim and was chased around by the fish for hours before his mother fished him out.

Then the big tortoise-shell cat almost mistook him for a mouse as he emerged from his exploration of the mousehole which she'd been watching all morning.

Another day, while he was playing in the long grass, he was almost swallowed by the black and white cow. But she quickly spat him out again when Tom battered sharply with his little fists on her tongue.

Nor was that the end of Tom's adventures.

One day Tom's mother was making a cake. Tom, ever curious, climbed up on the edge of the bowl when his mother wasn't looking. Standing on the edge, he leaned too far out and lost his balance. Down he fell into the mixture.

He tried to call out, but the batter got in his mouth and he couldn't say a word. He was baking in the oven before he could utter a word. For the first time in his life he felt frightened. He banged on the sides of the tin and jumped around.

The noise of the tin jumping about in the oven frightened his mother.

"This cake must be bewitched," thought the poor woman. And she threw it out of the window.

It landed in some bushes where a tinker found it later. He put it in his bag, intending to eat it for his supper.

But when he started to eat it he got quite a shock.

"Put me down! Put me down!" came a little voice.

Terrified, the poor man threw the cake down and ran for his life.

Just then a raven, flying overhead, saw something squirming on the ground. Thinking it might be a delicate morsel and feeling a bit peckish at the time, the raven picked Tom up in his beak. But, accustomed as he was to wriggly worms, the raven found Tom a much more troublesome mouthful. For Tom danced on the bird's tongue and punched his jaws. After a short struggle, the raven dropped Tom out of his beak, right in the middle of the sea.

Tom shot down through the clear blue water. Then, suddenly, darkness surrounded the boy. He guessed, and rightly, that he had been swallowed by a fish. But he was so seasick he lost all count of time.

The fish was soon caught and brought to the kitchen of the palace. So the next thing Tom knew the fish was slit open and, glad to be on dry land again, Tom climbed out . . . right in the middle of King Arthur's table.

How the King and his Knights laughed at the sight of the tiny boy standing on the edge of the big serving dish!

King Arthur was charmed by the gay little fellow, who also became a great favourite with all the knights and ladies of the court.

He was treated like a prince of the realm. A tiny golden castle was built for him in the king's gardens, complete with towers and moat, and he had his own golden chair in Arthur's throne room. When the king went riding Tom often sat in front of him on his great white charger, and the king had a specially made silk pouch hung on his belt so that Tom might rest in it when he felt weary.

Tom Thumb repaid all this kindness by bringing laughter and happiness into the sober life of the court. He was always up to some merry prank: hiding in somebody's pocket so that he might pinch and tease them, causing them to laugh most heartily when they should be most solemn; perching on the king's drinking goblet like a giant bee or, when he dared, coasting down Merlin's long white beard.

Now, in those days, great tournaments were held, in which the knights opposed each other on horseback, fighting with swords till one of them was thrown off his horse. Tom longed to join in this sport, so the fairies were called in consultation to see how this might be arranged.

After much discussion, it was decided that a white mouse should be trained to be Tom's faithful steed. The mouse was fitted with a bridle and saddle of the softest red leather. Tom himself was clad in a silver coat of armour. His sword was a darning needle fitted into a handle which was encrusted with tiny gems.

Now the little fellow could accompany the court on his own mount as they rode to hunt. So brave was he that, to the delight of the king, he even engaged in battle with opponents much bigger than himself, and he became the toast of the tournaments for his courage, and sometimes even for his victory.

But, as might be expected, some of the courtiers became jealous of the delight which Arthur took in his tiniest knight. And they plotted among themselves how they might bring him to disgrace.

Hearing their evil rumours and fearing that the king might believe them, Tom crawled into an empty snail shell one day and hid there until he was almost starved to death.

But as he lay there, hungry and dispirited, the intelligent little fellow thought about his problem and decided that this was indeed a foolish way to try to solve it. He must leave the king's court altogether; somewhere, in the kingdom, he would find a place to hide where he could live a simple life in safety.

So, venturing out, he spied a bright-winged butterfly. This would carry him at least part of the long journey, Tom thought, so he hopped on to the butterfly's back.

But the palace gardens were full of beautiful flowers and the butterfly was quite content to remain within the walls, flitting from flower to fragrant flower.

It so happened that, on this morning, King Arthur was taking a walk through his rose gardens when he spied the bright butterfly with its tiny passenger. He had been very concerned about Tom's disappearance and now, unless he caught him, the little fellow might be lost to him forever.

Immediately he began to chase the butterfly and soon the whole court joined in the pursuit.

Through the rose beds and the beautifully tended flower borders they scrambled; up and down the fruit trees; through the strawberry beds and over the wall where the vines climbed. The gardeners looked on in dismay and then they, too, dropped their tools to join in the chase.

The butterfly began to resent all this unwelcome attention, and at last he turned upside down in the air so that his little passenger was thrown off his back.

Down Tom fell, through the air and into the big watering can that one of the gardeners had just dropped. He would have surely drowned had not one of the pages seen him fall. He fished Tom out, dripping and gasping.

King Arthur and his court welcomed the tiny knight back with much joy and celebration, and even those who had been jealous of him before were glad to have him back again. He went back to live in his tiny golden castle, and his parents were given a house nearby.

From that day forth none dared harm Tom Thumb. By King Arthur's order, great Merlin protected the tiny person with his mighty powers. So Tom lived on, the smallest, but by no means the least famous, of King Arthur's court.